Good Morning to You, Valentine

♥ Poems for Valentine's Day ♥

Selected by Lee Bennett Hopkins
illustrated by Tomie de Paola

WORDSONG
BOYDS MILLS PRESS

Published by Wordsong
Boyds Mills Press, Inc.
A Highlights Company
815 Church Street
Honesdale, Pennsylvania 18431
Printed in Mexico

Publisher Cataloging-in-Publication Data
Main entry under title.
    Good morning to you, Valentine : poems for Valentine's Day /
selected by Lee Bennett Hopkins ; illustrations by Tomie de Paola.
[32] p. : ill. ; cm.
Includes index.
Originally published by Harcourt Brace Jovanovich in New York, 1976.
Summary: An anthology of twenty-three poems for Valentine's Day.
ISBN 1-878093-59-2
1. Saint Valentine's Day—Juvenile poetry. 2. Children's poetry. [1. Valentine's Day—Poetry.
2. Poetry—Collections.] I. Hopkins, Lee Bennett. II. de Paola, Tomie, ill. III. Title.
808 / .008—dc20   1993
Library of Congress Catalog Card Number: 91-70412

The text of this book is set in 11-point Galliard.
The illustrations are done in pen and ink.
Distributed by St. Martin's Press

10 9 8 7 6 5 4 3 2

To Barbara Lucas
   —with so much love!

Good Morning

Good morning to you, Valentine;
Curl your locks as I do mine,
One before and two behind,
Good morning to you, Valentine.

Anonymous

February

The sun rides higher
    Every trip.
The sidewalk shows.
    Icicles drip.

A snowstorm comes,
    And cars are stuck.
And ashes fly
    From the old town truck.

The chickadees
    Grow plump on seed
That Mother pours
    Where they can feed.

And snipping, snipping
    Scissors run
To cut out hearts
    For everyone.

John Updike

Somebody

Somebody loves you deep and true.
If I weren't so bashful, I'd tell you who.

Anonymous

Tomorrow is Saint Valentine's day,
  All in the morning betime,
And I a maid at your window
  To be your Valentine.

William Shakespeare

Valentine's Day

A cupid, a heart, and a dove,
And a sweet little message of love—
    Oh, that's what I got
    For the one who a lot
Of this day I have spent thinking *ove*.

Anonymous

Oh, Golden Heart

Oh, Golden Heart,
Be on your way.
Go, speed along
To sweetly say
That on this good
St. Valentine's Day
A heart is meant
To give away.

Anonymous

If I Were a Mailman

If I were a mailman,
  Know what I'd do?
I'd always bring mail
  With letters for YOU!

And on Valentine's Day
  I'd bring you plenty.
I might even bring you
  THREE HUNDRED AND TWENTY!

Vivian Gouled

A Sure Sign

Here's the mail, sort it quick—
Papers, letters, notes,
Postcard scenes,
Magazines;
Our hearts are in our throats.
Something there,
White and square,
Sealed with wax, and bumpy—
At the edges flat and thin,
In the middle lumpy.
When you feel the envelope,
Do your fingers trace
Something narrow,
Like an arrow?
Or a part
Of a heart?
Or a Cupid's face?
Is your name across the back
In a crooked line?
Hurry, then; that's a sign
Someone sent a valentine!

Nancy Byrd Turner

Valentine Feelings

I feel flippy,
I feel fizzy,
I feel whoopy,
I feel whizzy.

I'm feeling wonderful.
I'm feeling just fine.
Because you just gave me
A valentine.

Lee Bennett Hopkins

ME 4 U

Roses are red,
Violets are blue,
R U 4 me?
I am 4 U!

Anonymous

Read	See	That	Me
Read	see	that	me
up	will	I	love
and	you	love	you
down	and	you	and

Anonymous

I Love You

I love you, I love you,
I love you divine,
Please give me your bubble gum,
You're *sitting* on mine!

Anonymous

To My Valentine

If apples were pears,
And peaches were plums,
And the rose had a different name;
If tigers were bears,
And fingers were thumbs,
I'd love you just the same!

Anonymous

DANDELION

Conversation Hearts

In February, bring them home,
pink, yellow, lavender
and lime pastels
BE MINE   I'M YOURS
to be read by the tongue
that licks the chalk
and tastes what it spells.

I'll give you a boxful,
tasting of daphne, lupin,
mint and columbine;
a mouthful of secrets,
lovelier than whispers,
dear ones, friends
I'M YOURS   BE MINE

Nina Payne

BE MINE

I LOVE U

I LOVE YOU

"LUV:

FORGET ME NOT

KISS

R 4 U ME

I'M YOURS

SWEET

X X

Snowman's Valentine

Faye made a snowman, fat and fine,
And, oh, how his button eyes did shine
      When little Faye
      Gave him today
A big red heart for a valentine.

Kay Dee

Valentines

I gave a hundred Valentines.
A hundred, did I say?
I gave a *thousand* Valentines
one cold and wintry day.

I didn't put my name on them
or any other words,
because my Valentines were seeds
for February birds.

Aileen Fisher

Valentine from a Bird

Swinging high, high, high in the maple tree
Was the prettiest bird I ever did see,
    Chirping, "I love you,
    I do-do-do"—
A valentine love song—and all for me!

Anonymous

Valentine for Earth

Oh, it will be fine
To rocket through space
And see the reverse
Of the moon's dark face,

To travel to Saturn
Or Venus or Mars,
Or maybe discover
Some uncharted stars.

But do they have anything
Better than we?
Do you think, for instance,
They have a blue sea

For sailing and swimming?
Do the planets have hills
With raspberry thickets
Where a song sparrow fills

The summer with music?
And do they have snow
To silver the roads
Where the school buses go?

Oh, I'm all for rockets
And worlds cold or hot,
But I'm wild in love
With the planet we've got.

Frances Frost

The Best Valentine

Some valentines are paper,
Shaped like hearts of pink and gold.
Some valentines are flowers
In a soft green tissue fold.
Some valentines are candy,
But the one I got instead
Was a furry little puppy
With a collar that was red.

Margaret Hillert

A Love Song

Do I love you?
I'll tell you true.

Do chickens have lips?
Do pythons have hips?

Do penguins have arms?
Do spiders have charms?

Do oysters get colds?
Do leopards have moles?

Does a bird cage make a zoo?
Do I love you?

Raymond Richard Patterson

Question

Do you love me
Or do you not?
You told me once
But I forgot.

Anonymous

THE
JETS
LUV
FLORA

J.B.
+
M.P.

Valentine

I got a valentine from Timmy
                         Jimmy
                         Tillie
                         Billie
                         Nicky
                         Micky
                         Ricky
                         Dicky
                         Laura
                         Nora
                         Cora
                         Flora
                         Donnie
                         Ronnie
                         Lonnie
                         Connie
Eva even sent me two
But I didn't get *none* from you.

Shel Silverstein

29

Mix-up

I climbed up the door
And shut the stairs
I said my shoes
And took off my prayers.

I shut off the bed
And climbed into the light
And all because—
She kissed me Goodnight.

Anonymous

INDEX